Based on the TV series *Nickelodeon Avatar: The Last Airbender*™ as seen on Nickelodeon®

SIMON SPOTLIGHT
An imprint of Simon & Schuster Children's Publishing Division
1230 Avenue of the Americas, New York, New York 10020
© 2007 Viacom International Inc. All rights reserved. NICKELODEON, *Nickelodeon Avatar: The Last Airbender*, and all related titles, logos, and characters are trademarks of Viacom International Inc.
All rights reserved, including the right of reproduction in whole or in part in any form.
SIMON SPOTLIGHT and colophon are registered trademarks of Simon & Schuster, Inc.
Nontoxic
Manufactured in the United States of America
First Edition 1 2 3 4 5 6 7 8 9 10
ISBN-13: 978-1-4169-3829-3
ISBN-10: 1-4169-3829-X
Library of Congress Catalog Card Number 2007922923

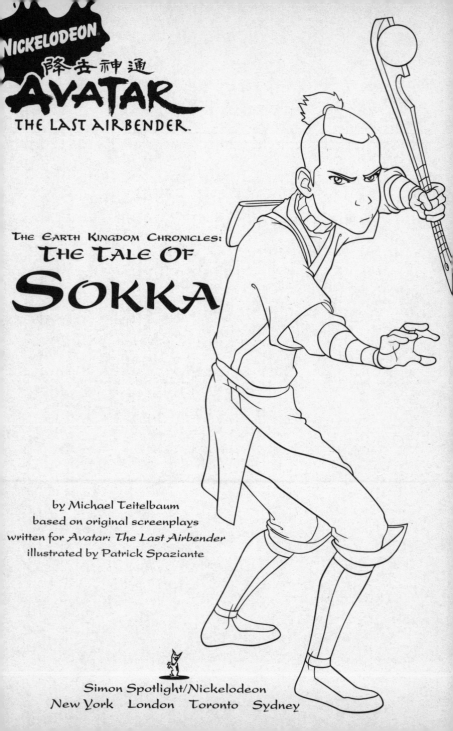

NICKELODEON

降击神通

AVATAR

THE LAST AIRBENDER.

THE EARTH KINGDOM CHRONICLES:
# THE TALE OF
# SOKKA

by Michael Teitelbaum
based on original screenplays
written for *Avatar: The Last Airbender*
illustrated by Patrick Spaziante

Simon Spotlight/Nickelodeon
New York   London   Toronto   Sydney

降壱神通

# Chapter 1

My name is Sokka. I'm a warrior from the Southern Water Tribe. My sister, Katara, and I have been traveling with Aang, the Avatar, for some time now. We're kind of his unofficial bodyguards. Katara is a Waterbender and she's been teaching Aang Waterbending. As a master of planning strategy, I'm here for my brains—and for my skill in battle with a boomerang.

We've just stopped a Fire Nation attack on the Water Tribes of the North Pole. Okay, so Aang really did most of the actual stopping, but Katara and I were right there to give our support.

While we were at the North Pole I met the most amazing girl in the world, Princess Yue. She was beautiful. And I say "was" because she became the moon to help save the Water Tribe. It was so sad. I was SO sad. . . . But she did the right thing.

Well, enough mushy stuff! I've got a job to do.

Aang has to travel to the Earth Kingdom next to begin learning Earthbending from his old pal King Bumi in the Earth Kingdom city of Omashu. You see, Aang has to master all four elements so he can stop the Fire Nation and end the war that's messed up the lives of so many people—including mine. My dad left home with other warriors from the Southern Water Tribe to fight the Fire Nation. Katara and I haven't seen him in a very long time, and I really, really miss him.

Aang, Katara, Momo (Aang's winged lemur), and I all climbed onto Appa (Aang's flying bison) and flew off toward Omashu. Our first stop was an Earth Kingdom base run by General Fong. This Fong guy was supposed to provide us with an escort to Omashu.

"Welcome, Avatar Aang!" Fong said when

we landed. "And welcome to all of you, great heroes. Appa, Momo, mighty Katara, and brave Sokka."

Now THIS guy had things figured out. He called me "brave Sokka!" Awesome.

But Fong had a strange idea: He wanted to force Aang into the Avatar state—where he gets amazingly powerful, but a little out of control—so he could defeat the Fire Lord quickly. Aang agreed with the general, but Katara didn't.

"Aang, there's a right way to do this," she said. "Practice, study, discipline."

That sounded pretty dull to me. "Or just glow it up and stomp that Fire Lord!" I countered.

"Katara, I don't have time to do this the right way!" Aang said.

Glow it up, here we come! But no matter how hard Fong tried, Aang just couldn't force himself into the Avatar state. And Fong went all nutso about it! He slammed Aang with an Earthbending blast, knocking him through a window! I couldn't believe this guy had just attacked Aang.

Before I could do anything, Fong's soldiers grabbed me, which made me even madder. I struggled to break free of the soldiers' grasp, then rushed to help Aang.

At that moment, Fong made the ground in the courtyard open up and swallow Katara.

"Katara! No!" I called out.

That's when Aang's fury made him slip into the Avatar state. Come on, buddy, you've got to rescue Katara!

He whipped up a huge funnel of wind that knocked aside Fong and his soldiers. Boy, Aang is really scary looking when he's like that.

8 "Katara is really in no danger," Fong admitted. "Burying her in the ground was just a trick to get Aang mad."

Well it sure worked! And just like that, Katara was freed. But Fong wasn't satisfied. That guy was really out of his mind.

"That was almost perfect!" he shouted as Katara comforted Aang. "We just have to find a way to control you when you're like that. I guess we'll figure it out on the way to the Fire Nation."

Uh-uh. There was no way the general was coming with us to the Fire Nation. As far as I was concerned, the only place he was going to was dreamland.

I sneaked up behind Fong and bopped him on the helmet with my boomerang.

WAP! Down he went for a nice little nap.

"Anybody got a problem with that?" I asked, looking around at Fong's troops. Not surprisingly, no one protested.

Next stop, Omashu!

We stopped by a river for a short rest.

From out of nowhere I heard music. Looking up I saw a group of weird-looking people coming from the woods. They played musical instruments and sang. Hmm . . . they seemed friendly, but these days you never know. The Fire Nation is tricky and they've got lots of spies everywhere. I wouldn't put it past them to be working in disguise to throw us off.

I confronted these so-called musicians. "Who are you?"

"I'm Chong, and this is my wife, Lily," said a guy with long hair and flowers around his neck. "We're nomads, happy to go wherever the wind takes us."

Nomads, huh? Could be. But how would we know for sure?

"I'm a nomad too," Aang said.

"Hey, me too!" Chong replied.

"I know. You just said that," Aang said.

Okay, so they couldn't be spies. The guy seemed too out of it to be from the Fire Nation!

Chong started telling Aang stories about all the places he'd been. While that's all very nice, we had someplace we needed to be. "Look, I hate to be the wet blanket here, but we need to get to Omashu quickly. No sidetracks," I said.

"Omashu is dangerous. Maybe you should go someplace else," Chong chimed in.

What's with this guy? We're not tourists looking for a fun vacation spot. We're on a mission. A very important mission. "We're going to Omashu!" I repeated.

"Whoa! Sounds like someone's got a case of destination fever. You worry too much about where you're going."

Maybe he didn't hear me right, so I repeated, louder this time, "O-MA-SHU!"

Then Katara explained that we needed to find King Bumi so that Aang could learn Earthbending.

"Sounds like you guys are headed to Omashu," Chong said, like it was the first time he had heard of our plan.

I smacked my forehead in frustration. "That's what I've been trying to tell you all along!" This guy was really dense.

Then Chong told us about a secret tunnel that leads right through the mountain. A short—cut to Omashu carved by two lovers who were the first Earthbenders.

"I think we'll just stick with flying," I said. "We've dealt with the Fire Nation before. We'll be fine."

We took off on Appa, but a few minutes into our flight the Fire Nation attacked, shooting huge fireballs at us and trying to knock us from the sky. Okay, this was way more than we'd faced before. And Appa was freaking out from the fire. We had to turn back. "Secret tunnel, here we come!"

"Actually, it's not just one tunnel," Chong told us when we returned to the river. "It's a whole labyrinth."

"A labyrinth?" I asked. A series of twisting paths built so that anyone who entered would get hopelessly lost inside forever? Great plan, Chong! Maybe those fireballs weren't that hot after all.

"It'll be fun, Sokka," Aang said, smiling that cheery, optimistic smile he always has.

Fun? Oh, sure, getting lost in an endless maze, being stuck in the dark, and being trapped with no food is definitely my idea of a good time! Not.

At that moment I spotted smoke in the sky. "It's the Fire Nation. They're tracking us. Everyone into the tunnels," I said.

The nomads lit five torches so we could find our way in the dark. Now it was up to me. I'm the plan guy. All we needed was a plan. "Chong, how long do those torches last?"

"Two hours each."

"We have five torches, so that means we have ten hours of light!" Lily said.

I smacked my forehead again. These nomads sure were completely clueless. I tried to be patient as I explained, "It doesn't work like that if they're all lit at the same time!"

Suddenly a wolf–bat came flying right at Katara. I swung my torch at the creature, but the torch slipped from my hand and rolled toward Appa.

The fire freaked Appa out and he started jumping around and slamming his tail into the wall. Unfortunately, the force of Appa's tail shook loose rocks from the ceiling, and they came tumbling down all around us.

The next thing I knew I was flying backward through the air. When I landed, I saw that a huge wall of rock had fallen between me and Aang, Katara, and Appa. Aang must have pushed me to safety with an Airbending blast.

Oh, boy, now I was trapped on the side of the rock wall with Momo and those annoying singing nomads! I began pulling rocks off the pile, trying to break through.

"It's no use," Chong said. "We're separated. But at least you have us."

"Noooo!" I was not going to spend whatever time was left in my life with those smiling, singing, clueless nomads! I picked up my pace, digging though the rocks faster and faster, but all I succeeded in doing was bringing more rocks down from above. It was no use. I had to find another way out.

As we moved further through the tunnels, the nomads began singing, "Don't let the cave-in get you down . . ."

"I don't get it," I said. "You guys travel around the world with no maps and no idea of where you're going. How do you ever get anywhere?"

"Somewhere is everywhere, and so you never really need to get anywhere because you're already here," Chang said.

"Don't remind me," I said, almost ready to admit defeat. I know I'm here! That's the problem. I don't want to be here, I want to be there, which is where I'm not. Oh, great—I was starting to sound like them.

That's when I heard wolf-bats howl again.

We kept moving, but I was completely lost. It was strange. I had a feeling the tunnels were constantly changing, because once again we hit a dead end. But how could they be changing?

"Your plans have led us to a dead end," said a nomad named Moku.

"At least I'm trying to get us out of here!" I replied impatiently.

Then a flock of wolf-bats swarmed us. I

swatted at the bats with my boomerang, but amazingly they all just flew right past us.

"Sokka, you saved us!" Chong said.

"No, they didn't leave because of me," I said, realizing what was happening. "They were fleeing."

"Fleeing? From what?"

A low roar filled the caves. "From whatever is making that noise!"

Suddenly the cave wall burst open and giant badger-moles rushed out.

I was right! The tunnels were changing because the badger-moles were digging new ones all the time. But being right didn't do much good if I wasn't going to make it out of there to tell anyone.

As one humongous creature came at me, I tripped and fell backward. My hand hit the strings of one of the nomad's instruments and it made a musical sound, which caused a very strange thing to happen: The badger-mole stopped charging and actually looked friendly.

Badger-moles. Music. Digging. That's it! Sokka's got a plan!

"Quick, start playing," I shouted to the nomads. "Play anything, as long as it's music!"

They made up a song about the badger-moles, but it really didn't make any difference what they were singing about. As long as they made music, the badger-moles stayed friendly. So friendly, in fact, that they let us climb up onto their backs as they tunneled through the mountain.

A while later, with me leading and the nomads singing, the badger-moles burst

through the far side of the mountain.

We made it—we were out! The nomads turned out to be good for something after all.

Aang, Katara, and Appa were waiting for us. "How did you guys get out?" I asked.

"Like the legend says, we let love lead the way," Aang said.

Okay, that sounds corny, but whatever. "Really? We let huge ferocious beasts lead our way," I bragged.

"Why is your forehead all red?" Katara asked me, but I didn't explain.

"Nobody react to what I'm about to tell you,"

Chong whispered as he pointed at Aang. "I think that kid might be the Avatar."

I slapped my forehead in disbelief one more time, and Katara understood why it was red.

We said our good—byes and continued on our way to Omashu. As we reached the top of a hill I pulled out my telescope to get my first look at the great Earth Kingdom city.

"I present to you the Earth Kingdom city of O—Oh, no!" I couldn't believe what I was seeing. A huge Fire Nation flag was hanging from the city's main wall. How could this have happened? How could the Fire Nation have taken over Omashu? And what about King Bumi?

Our journey just got a whole lot tougher.

# Chapter 2

What do we do now?

Aang was really upset. "Omashu always seemed untouchable," he said.

"Up until now it was," I said. "Now Ba Sing Se is the only great Earth Kingdom stronghold left."

"This is horrible," Katara said, "but we have to move on."

"No," Aang insisted.

"There are other people who can teach you Earthbending, Aang," she pointed out.

"This isn't about finding a teacher. It's about finding my friend."

Hard to argue with that, but we still had one little problem. How did we get inside? We couldn't exactly stroll into an occupied city and ask to see the king, who may or may not still be in power.

That's when Aang found a secret passage—way. Actually, it was a filthy, slime–ridden sewer. Aang opened the entrance and a wave of thick, green muck came pouring out.

Oh, man, it was the most disgusting thing I've ever smelled! I thought I was going to be sick.

Aang used Airbending to create a bubble for us to walk in as we made our way along the sewer pipe, but for some reason I still came out com—pletely covered in stinky muck at the other end.

The things I have to do to win a war.

We popped out of a manhole on a quiet street in the city and I could barely breathe. Katara washed the muck off me with a Waterbending move, then Aang dried me off with an Airbending wind. That's when I noticed the little round, purple bug–type things attached to my face. "I'm doomed!" I yelled. "Some horrible poisonous sewer bugs are sucking the brains from my head! Help! Get them off! Ahh!"

"Stop making so much noise," Aang scolded, reaching out for one of the bugs. "It's just a purple pentapus."

Aang gently tickled one of the hideous leeches with his finger and it let go. As he was freeing the creatures, a group of Fire Nation soldiers showed up. Uh—oh.

"What are you kids doing out past curfew?" one of them asked.

Curfew? The Fire Nation has imposed a curfew on the city? This was horrible. I struggled to come up with a good answer fast, but Katara beat me to it.

20

"We were just on our way home," she replied.

Not great, but at least it's an answer.

Then a Fire Nation soldier pointed at me and asked, "What's the matter with him?"

What? What did he mean? What's wrong with me? What was he talking about?

"He has pentapox, sir," Katara said. "That's what those spots are on his face."

Spots? On my face? What is SHE talking about?

"It's highly contagious," Katara continued.

I finally got it. Those purple whatchamacallits

must have left spots on my face. It was time for a little acting.

"It's so awful!" I moaned in my best sick-guy voice. I can be a great actor. "I'm dying! Dying!"

"It's also deadly," Katara added.

Now for a little more moaning and coughing. Ah, the soldiers have taken off! They're scared. Pentapox. Good one, Katara. And not a bad performance on my part, either.

We continued along the streets. It was weird. Last time we were here this was a busy city with people everywhere. Now it's like a ghost town. Must be the curfew.

Then from out of nowhere a family came strolling down the empty street, guarded by more Fire Nation soldiers. They must be important people. Just before I could figure out who they were, a low rumbling noise filled the air.

I looked up and saw large boulders rolling down Omashu's mail chutes, heading straight for the family, which included a teenage girl and a young boy.

Aang moved quickly, Airbending the boulders away from the family. To our surprise, the woman cried out, "The resistance!"

The teenage daughter immediately began flinging flying daggers at Aang—at all of us, in fact! What a way to show gratitude.

So the good news was that there must be some kind of organized resistance to the Fire Nation's takeover of the city. The bad news was that the girl with the special daggers thought we were part of it! And she's got good aim!

It was time to run!

As a dozen flying daggers zipped our way, the ground beneath us suddenly began  to drop, and then stopped abruptly. We fell to the ground, and when I rubbed the dust out of my eyes I saw that we were underground, surrounded by a bunch of Earth Kingdom people. These guys were the resistance. They saved us.

"So is King Bumi with you guys?" Aang asked. "Is he leading the resistance?"

The look of surprise on everyone's faces was unexpected.

"Of course not," the resistance leader said. "On the day of the invasion King Bumi surrendered."

He WHAT? Now this Bumi guy is a little crazy, but he's an old friend of Aang's and I can't imagine anyone Aang trusts giving up his city so easily. But that's apparently what happened.

"It doesn't matter now," the resistance leader added. "Fighting the Fire Nation is the only path to freedom."

"Actually, there's another path to freedom," Aang replied. "You could leave Omashu."

The Earthbenders gave us another surprised look, but they were willing to hear us out. It was my job to come up with a plan, something that would make the Fire Nation WANT everyone to leave.

"You're all about to come down with a nasty case of pentapox."

Throughout the city, Earth Kingdom citizens put pentapi on their faces and arms causing red spots to appear. "The spots make you look sick, but you have to act sick too," I advised.

I gave them a few pointers, and then we were ready to put my brilliant plan into action. "Okay, everyone into the sick formation. Let's go!"

Wouldn't you know it, the Fire Nation governor

bought our scheme completely! He ordered all the "infected" people out of the city, but Aang stayed behind to find Bumi. I guess it doesn't matter what Bumi did to his city, Aang will stay loyal to his friend—even if he is insane!

I helped the others set up camp just outside the city. Aang returned a while later, with no news about Bumi. Then we discovered we had another problem. The little boy whose family we had saved earlier from the boulders had followed us out, and it turns out that it was the family of the Fire Nation governor!

24

The governor's son is cute, but he insisted on playing with my boomerang like it was a toy. "No. Bad Fire Nation baby!" I scolded.

I took it away from him and he started screaming. I gave in. "Oh, all right. Here."

Just then a messenger hawk flew into our camp with a scroll.

"It's from the governor," Aang said. "He thinks we took his son. He wants to make a trade—his son for King Bumi."

Even though this seemed too convenient to me, Aang, Katara, and I headed back into the city with the kid.

"You realize we're probably walking into a trap," I said.

"I don't think so," Aang said. Sometimes he can be a little too trusting.

When we arrived at the meeting place, we were surprised that the governor was not there. Instead there were three girls, including one I recognized as the governor's daughter—the one with the flying daggers. I'd better keep my eyes wide open and my boomerang ready.

They lowered Bumi down on a chain. He was stuck in a metal container—totally Earthbending-proof. Then the governor's daughter stepped forward.

"The deal's off," she announced. Uh, did I miss something? What happened?

As Bumi's box rose up, the governor's daughter began flinging her daggers. I was right. This was a trap!

"We've got to get the baby out of here!" Katara cried.

"Way ahead of you!" I replied, dashing away with the kid.

Signaling for Appa to get us out, I blew on Aang's bison whistle when someone tripped me.

I skidded toward the edge of the high platform, but managed to stop before we fell off.

Then, hopping onto Appa's back, I flew around to help Katara just as one of the girls—Ty Lee—pinched her, cutting off her chi and her ability to bend.

The governor's daughter, whose name was Mai, pulled out a three-prong dagger. "How are you going to fight without your bending?" she taunted Katara.

I could not believe she said that. Like only benders can fight. Obviously she'd never met ME before. I flung my boomerang at the girl, knocking the dagger from her hand. "I seem to manage," I said.

I helped Katara onto Appa and we flew to get Aang, who had been fighting off the third girl and trying to rescue Bumi. He didn't get Bumi, but at least he got rid of the girl.

Aang returned the little guy to his parents. I'm going to miss the kid. Well, except for the whole boomerang—touching thing.

# Chapter 3

As we flew over the Earth Kingdom I glanced down and saw that we were right above a thick, swampy forest. Suddenly a huge tornado came out of nowhere!

"Faster! We've got to go faster!" I called, but it was no use. We were going down!

The tornado tossed us around and around and we finally splashed down into the swamp. Katara and Aang landed next to me, but there were no signs of Appa or Momo. They could be anywhere in the thick tangle of vines, roots, and branches. Fortunately, I had the right tool for dealing with unruly forests—a machete.

"Maybe we should be a little nicer to the swamp," Aang said as I started hacking away.

"Aang, these are just plants," I said, not bothering to stop.

That night we made camp and quickly dozed off. But before I could fall into deep sleep, something woke me up. It was a vine! It had a tight hold of my ankle and was pulling me deeper into the jungle. I had to slice my way free and run, but wouldn't you know it, the vines started chasing me!

The swamp was alive. "I'm sorry, swamp, I'm sorry, but please don't drag me into the murky water," I said. Then it let go of me.

"Stupid swamp," I muttered. I had to find the others to tell them what happened, but I stumbled and plopped down into the muck. Then I heard someone calling my name. "Hello? Is there anyone there?" I called back.

I looked up toward the voice and couldn't believe my eyes. A ghostly image floated above the swamp. It was Yue, princess of the Northern Water Tribe. A girl I really cared about. And who I couldn't save at the North Pole. No, it couldn't be her. That's impossible. Yue was gone—forever.

This was just a trick of the light, or swamp gas. I rubbed my eyes and took a deep breath—and Yue was still there.

"You didn't protect me," she said, and disappeared. I felt even more sad and alone. I miss you, Yue. I'm sorry I let you down.

I continued wandering through the stupid swamp for what seemed like forever. Then I heard a noise. Something was coming toward me. I tightened my grip on the machete, and— OOF! Whatever it was just crashed into me.

"Aang! Katara! What are you doing? I've been looking all over for you!" I exclaimed, excited to see them.

"I was chasing some girl," Aang said.

"I thought I saw Mom," Katara added.

"Look we were all just scared and hungry and our minds were playing tricks on us," I told them. "That's why we all saw things."

"All our visions led us here," Aang said, a little too knowingly.

"Okay, so where is 'here'?"

"It's the heart of the swamp. It's been calling to us."

Okay, this was some of that creepy,

magical Avatar stuff that I have a hard time buying. If I can't see something, eat something, or battle something, I don't believe in it.

Suddenly a huge swamp monster rose up from the water and attacked us! After a long battle, with me slashing and Aang and Katara bending, we discovered that it was just a Waterbender bending the water in the vines.

"See? Completely reasonable," I said to Aang. "Not a monster. Just a guy defending his home."

"This whole swamp is actually just one tree, spread out over miles," the Waterbender explained. "The tree is one big living organism. Just like the entire world."

Oh, great. More magical, mystical Avatar stuff. But when Aang touched the huge tree, he had a vision of Appa and Momo. He saw where they were.

We wasted no time in rescuing them from some local Waterbenders and finally got out of the swamp. If I never see another one again it'll be too soon!

We arrived in the Earth Kingdom town of Gaoling. A guy on the street handed us a flyer for Master Yu's Earthbending Academy, and it had a coupon good for one free Earthbending lesson.

"Maybe this could be the Earthbending teacher you're looking for," Katara said to Aang.

But the guy at the academy turned out to be a sleazebag. All he was interested in was getting Aang's money. Then we heard about an Earthbending tournament, called Earth Rumble Six, where the best Earthbenders in the world would be competing.

It was kind of a win—win thing. Aang would get to see the best Earthbenders, hoping that one of them might be able to teach him, and I would get to be in the crowd for the sporting event of the year.

After a few preliminary matches, the champion came out—and it was a young girl who was blind! She called herself the Blind Bandit. How in the world did she become the champ?

"She can't really be blind," Katara said. "It's just part of her character, right?"

"I think she is," Aang said.

"I think she's going down!" I said.

But no, she fought hard, Earthbending like crazy and beating a guy called the Boulder, who was three times her size. It was amazing!

After that defeat, the guy who ran the tournament, Xin Fu, made an announcement. "I'm offering this sack of gold to anyone who can defeat the Blind Bandit!" There was silence. "What? No one dares to face her?" he taunted the crowd.

All of a sudden Aang jumped into the ring. "I will!" he shouted.

"Go, Aang! Avenge the Boulder!" If anyone could beat the Blind Bandit, it would be Aang. He was going to wipe her out!

But then Aang said the weirdest thing to the Blind Bandit. "I don't want to fight you. I want to talk to you," he said.

Okay, Aang, you have lost your mind. No talking! We're here to win! Well, the Blind Bandit didn't want to talk, anyway. She just wanted to fight. So they finally fought, and Aang beat her. All right, Aang! As his manager, I jumped into the ring and snatched up the sack of gold.

"Way to go, champ!" I exclaimed loudly.

Later, Aang told me that he thought the Blind Bandit was the Earthbending teacher he had been looking for.

"She was the girl in my vision in the swamp," he explained.

Apparently when Aang was trying to rescue Bumi, the former Earth King had told him to find an Earthbending teacher who waited and listened. "That's what the Blind Bandit did to beat all those other guys," Aang added excitedly. "We've got to find her!"

So we tracked the girl to this amazing "rich people" estate. You know, huge house, sprawling gardens. We're talking big bucks. Some family called the Beifongs. We snuck onto the grounds and surprised the girl, the Blind Bandit.

I guess she wasn't too happy about it because the next moment the ground shot up under my feet. How in the world did she do that?

"What are you doing here?" the girl demanded.

"Well, a crazy king told me I had to find an Earthbender who listens to the earth," Aang explained. "Then I had a vision in a magic swamp and—"

Katara took over. "What Aang is trying to say is that he's the Avatar, and if he doesn't master Earthbending soon he won't be able to defeat the Fire Lord."

"Not my problem," the Blind Bandit said. "Now get out of here or I'll call the guards."

She didn't realize how wrong she was! It's obvious people like her are going to wait until the Fire Nation breaks down their doors before they realize that this war affects all of us. "Look, we all have to do our part to win this war, and yours is teaching Aang Earthbending," I insisted.

"Guards!" she screamed.

We immediately scrambled back over the wall. Okay, time to come up with a way to convince her that we are not crazy, that we have a truly important mission.

Aang came up with a plan. I know, that's usually my job, but occasionally I like to let other people share in a bit of glory. We went right up to the front door and announced that the Avatar was here to see the very important Beifong family. It worked! We were invited in for dinner. Not bad, Aang.

Sometimes being with the Avatar has its perks.

The Blind Bandit, whose real name is Toph, was not pleased to see us. Especially when Aang tried his best to convince her why she had to be his teacher. And then, get this, we find out that Toph's parents have no idea she's the Blind Bandit! They don't know that she's a great Earthbender. They think she's a helpless little blind girl!

We were completely taken aback. Every time Aang tried to point out how good she is, she kicked him with an Earthbending shot under the table. Weird.

Later that night Toph came to our room. Aang thought she wanted to fight.

"Relax," she said. "Look, I'm sorry about dinner. Let's call a truce, okay?"

"What's the catch?" Aang asked suspiciously.

"I just want to talk." The two of them headed outside.

Fine by me. I settled down in my cushy bed for a good night's sleep.

But not for long. Someone burst into the room to tell Katara and me that Aang and

Toph had been captured. We rushed outside, where I found a piece of paper.

"Whoever took Aang and Toph left this," I said.

"A ransom note!" Katara said. "It says, 'If you want to see your daughter again bring five hundred gold pieces to the arena.' It's signed by Xin Fu and the Boulder."

Hurrying back to the Earthbending arena with Toph's father, we found Aang and Toph trapped in cages! They were surrounded by Xin Fu and a bunch of Earthbenders.

36

"Here's your money," I said furiously, tossing the sack of gold to the ground. "Now let them go."

Xin Fu let Toph go, but he decided to keep Aang. "The Fire Nation will pay a hefty price for the Avatar. Now get out of my ring."

I was not about to let him get away with that. Still, I didn't know if Katara and I could take all these Earthbenders by ourselves. We needed Toph, but she was standing with her dad. What was she going to do? Would she let them take Aang to protect her precious little secret, or would she help us with some white–

hot Earthbending moves?

"Toph, we need you," Katara pleaded.

"My daughter is blind and helpless," said Toph's father. "She cannot help you."

"Yes, I can!" Toph said. And boy, did she help. All right . . . she did it all herself.

Toph put on an amazing demonstration of Earthbending. She knocked all the other Earthbenders, including Xin Fu himself, right out of the ring.

I still don't know how she does all that without seeing.

After we freed Aang, he explained that Toph sees using Earthbending. She uses her feet to feel the vibrations caused by any movement. I was impressed.

Now things should be great for Toph because her father knows what an awesome Earthbender she really is. But instead of being proud of her, he was angry!

"I've let you have far too much freedom," Toph's father told her when we were back at his house. "From now on you will be cared for and guarded twenty-four hours a day!"

What was his problem? He has a daughter

who's an amazing Earthbender, and he just wants to keep her locked up? I don't get it. He should want to show off her gift.

"Toph needs freedom to see the world and experience new things," Aang said.

Toph's father didn't even bother responding to Aang. He told his guards sternly, "Please escort the Avatar and his friends out. They are no longer welcome here."

I couldn't believe he was kicking us out! Oh, well. Good–bye, cushy bed.

"I'm sorry, Toph," Aang said.

"Good–bye, Aang," she replied sadly.

But a short while later, as we were preparing to leave on Appa, Toph came running up to us.

"My dad changed his mind," she said. "He said I was free to see the world."

Mr. Beifong didn't seem like the kind of guy who would change his mind so quickly, but I wasn't about to ask any questions. I was glad she was coming with us. Now Aang could learn Earthbending.

"We'd better leave before your dad changes his mind again," I said.

# Chapter 4

It was late afternoon when we landed in a small clearing in a wooded area. We began unloading our supplies to set up camp.

"Hey, you guys picked a great campsite," Toph said. "The grass is so soft."

"That's not grass," I pointed out. "Appa's shedding." His fur was all over the place.

That night Toph suddenly rushed out of her tent. "There's something coming toward us!"

We couldn't see anything, but we trusted Toph. We packed up all our stuff and climbed onto Appa's back before flying away just in time.

Sure enough, from above, we spotted a strange-looking metal tank chugging beneath us. We found another clearing and landed. And once again we unloaded our supplies and set up camp.

All this work, and I was so tired. Then Katara and Toph started arguing. Toph didn't want to unload or set up camp.

"Ever since you joined us you've been nothing but selfish and unhelpful!" Katara shouted.

"What?" Toph screamed. "Look here, sugar queen, I gave up everything to teach Aang Earthbending, so don't talk to me about being selfish."

"Sugar queen?" Katara repeated, shocked at what Toph had called her.

I laughed. Sugar queen. I have to give Toph credit for that one!

"Should we do something?" Aang asked me, a little concerned.

"Hey, I'm just enjoying the show," I said. It's better not to get involved with two angry girls.

But the arguing continued. "Hey, how's a guy supposed to sleep with all this yelling and earthquaking?" I said.

And wouldn't you know it, that tank thing came back, so we had to pack up and leave AGAIN. I didn't know when I would get to sleep—if ever!

Our next campsite was on the side of a tall mountain. Now I was officially exhausted. The bags under my eyes had bags. I had no plans to set up camp. All I wanted to do was stretch out on the softest pile of dirt I could find and go to sleep. I thought I could finally relax without worrying about that tank following us.

Then Toph jumped up.

"Oh, no! Don't tell me," I whined.

"Let's get out of here," Katara said, but Aang had a different plan this time.

"Maybe we should face them," he said. "Who knows, maybe they're friendly."

I sighed. "You're always the optimist, Aang." Nobody would go to all that trouble in a big scary-looking machine just to say, "Hi, how ya doing? Why don't we be friends?"

And a couple of minutes later I was proven right. The tank appeared and from its belly came those three crazy girls who fought us in Omashu, charging toward us on their mongoose-dragons.

It was clear they weren't coming to bring us a housewarming gift for our new campsite!

"We can take them," Toph announced, setting herself in a battle stance. "Three on three!"

Uh, I know she's blind and everything, but . . . I had to correct her. "Actually Toph, there's four of us."

"Oh, sorry," she said, not sounding sorry at all. "I didn't count you. You know, no bending and all."

And I was actually starting to like having her around! "I can still fight!" I snapped.

42

"Okay," she relented. "Three on three— plus Sokka."

Now I understood why Katara was arguing with her all the time! She knows how to make people mad.

The crazy girls continued to charge toward us. Toph created a wall of rock to stop them, but that didn't pose a problem. The Firebending girl just blasted the rock away and kept on coming. I have to say that she was one scary-looking Firebender! I had seen enough—I didn't need a closer look.

"Let's get out of here!" I yelled.

We got back on Appa and returned to the sky.

"I can't believe those girls followed us all the way from Omashu!" Katara said. "The crazy blue Firebending and the flying daggers are bad enough, but the last time we saw them, one of those girls did something that took my bending away. That's scary!"

I was exhausted. We were all exhausted, even Appa. And then, as if to prove the point, Appa fell asleep in midair, and we started to plunge toward the ground. We screamed. This was not the time to fall asleep!

"Appa's exhausted," Aang said. "We have to land." And so we set down near a river.

"Okay, we've put a lot of distance between us and them," I said when we landed. "The plan right now is to get some sleep!"

That's when Katara and Toph started up again. "Of course we could've gotten some sleep earlier if Toph didn't have such issues about helping," Katara said.

"What?" Toph cried. "You're blaming ME for this? If there's anyone to blame, it's Sheddy over there."

She pointed at Appa. "You want to know how they keep finding us? He's leaving a trail of fur everywhere we go!"

"How dare you blame Appa!" Aang shouted. "He saved your life three times today!"

Okay . . . I see there's not going to be any sleep for me anytime soon.

"Appa never had a problem flying when it was just the three us," Aang added harshly.

And all of a sudden it got really quiet. No one said anything and no one did anything—until Toph picked up her bags. "See ya," she said, as she headed toward the woods.

This was not good. We needed her. Aang needed her. I had to stop her.

"Wait!" I called out. But Toph pushed me away as she disappeared into the forest. I shot a look at Aang and Katara.

Nice going, guys. You blew off your Earthbending teacher and our early warning system for those psycho girls following us in their nasty tank.

"What did I just do?" Aang cried. "I yelled at my Earthbending teacher . . . and now she's gone."

"I was so mean to her," Katara added.

"Yeah, you two were pretty much jerks," I said.

"We need to find Toph and apologize," Katara said. I agreed, but I also had a question: "What are we going to do about the tank full of dangerous ladies chasing us?"

Aang came up with a plan. "You guys take Momo and Appa and go find Toph," he said. "I'm going to use some of Appa's fur to make a fake trail and lead the tank off course."

It was a good idea, but the crazy girls figured out the plan. Plus, Appa was just too tired to fly fast enough or high enough to avoid being spotted. So we soon saw two of the girls riding their mongoose-dragons, hot on our trail.

The girl from Omashu started throwing her flying daggers at me, but I was able to defend myself with my boomerang and club. Katara faced off with the girl who had blocked her chi before. We both fought hard, but in the end, it was Appa who saved us with an awesome Airbending move. Then we got out of there quick!

We caught up with Aang in a deserted town. He was being attacked by the Firebending girl. Zuko and his uncle were there too. We quickly landed and joined the battle.

Then, just when the Firebending girl was about to unleash one of her powerful blue lightning attacks, Toph showed up and knocked her to the ground with an Earthbending move.

"I thought you guys could use a little help," Toph said. I don't know what made her change her mind, but I was so happy she came back. We all surrounded the Firebender, who turned out to be Zuko's sister, Princess Azula! Great.

"Well, look at this," Azula cackled. "Enemies and traitors all working together. I'm done. I know when I'm beaten. A princess surrenders with honor."

It looked like she was going to surrender. She bowed her head, then all of a sudden, she blasted her uncle! This prompted everyone to immediately unleash attacks at her. But when the smoke cleared, she was gone.

Zuko ran to his uncle's side. The man was badly hurt, but it looked like he was going to make it.

"Zuko, I can help," Katara said, ready to use her healing ability.

"Get away from me!" Zuko shouted, before unleashing a fire blast just above our heads. "Leave!"

He didn't have to tell us twice. I was ready to go. And there was only one way to end this crazy long day. Appa flew us to a mountain ledge where we all stretched out and finally fell into a wonderful, deep sleep.

# Chapter 5

**48** After many days of traveling, we stopped for a rest on an open prairie.

Everyone felt like we needed a break. Aang had been training hard, practicing both Earthbending and Waterbending. So everyone chose a vacation spot. Everyone except me, that is.

"There's no time for vacations, Aang," I said. "Even if you do master all of the elements, then what? It's not like we have a map of the Fire Nation. We need information. We need intelligence. And we're not going to get that taking vacations."

I was voted down, of course. What a shock. I was the only one who wasn't either teaching or learning. Mr. Not-A-Bender here.

Next, for Katara's vacation, we traveled to some place called Misty Palms Oasis.

Well, the "oasis" was actually a dump— a rundown cantina with some lowlife Sandbenders hanging around like annoying bugs. Good choice, Katara. This was way more important than planning our strategy against the Fire Nation.

But it was in that flea trap that we met Professor Zei, an anthropologist and professor from Ba Sing Se University. He was searching for a lost library run by some spirit called Wan Shi Tong. The place was supposed to have books from all over the world, which meant that they might have some useful information or maps of the Fire Nation.

"For my vacation, I choose finding that library," I said eagerly.

Off we went, flying on Appa, with the professor guiding the way. We flew over the desert, which was one vast sea of brown. There was nothing but sand for miles. . . . Then I spotted something sticking out of the sand. "Down there. What's that?"

We landed and found a tower jutting out from the sand. I looked at Professor Zei's picture of the enormous library and realized that the thing we were looking at was the top spire of the building! "This is the library," I announced. "But it's completely buried in the sand!"

Toph used Earthbending to determine that the inside of the library was still completely intact, then we climbed up the spire and slipped in through a window. We left Toph to wait outside with Appa.

The place was huge! I had a really good feeling that we were going to find what we needed on the Fire Nation.

And then an enormous owl showed up.

"Are you the spirit who brought this library into the physical world?" I asked.

"Indeed. I am Wan Shi Tong, and you are obviously humans, who, by the way, are no longer permitted in the library."

"What do you have against humans?" Aang asked.

"Humans only bother learning things to get the edge on other humans. So who are you trying to destroy?"

Uh . . . how did he know? Was it written on our faces? I had to fake him out. "No, no destroying. We have come here to seek knowl—edge for knowledge's sake." Yes, that's a pretty good answer.

But the owl wasn't so easily fooled. "If you are going to lie to an all—knowing spirit being, you should at least put a little effort into it," he said.

I had to cover fast. "I'm not lying," I said. "I'm here with the Avatar, and he's the bridge between our worlds. He'll vouch for me."

"We will not abuse your library, good spirit. You have my word," Aang assured him.

I held my breath as we all waited for his response.

"Very well," the spirit said.

Whew! Now we just had to find something that would help us defeat the Fire Nation.

What I found was even more than I could have hoped for. First I discovered a burned scrap of paper with a date and the words "The Darkest Day in Fire Nation History." Then one of the owl's assistants, a fox, led us to a mechanical planetarium that showed the position of the sun, moon, and stars on any given day. Using this amazing machine we figured out that the date on the paper was the date of a solar eclipse—a day when the moon blocks out the sun. And during a solar eclipse, Firebenders lose their bending abilities.

This was it! This was the way to beat the Fire Nation!

"We just have to figure out when the next solar eclipse is happening," I told the others. "Then we've got to get that information to Ba Sing Se so the Earth King can plan to invade the Fire Nation on that day. The Fire Lord is going down!"

Just then there was an uncomfortable silence and I felt someone behind me. When I spun around, I saw the owl towering over us.

"Mortals are so predictable," the owl said. "And such terrible liars. You betrayed my trust."

"We're just trying to protect the people we love," I replied.

"And I'm going to protect what I love. I'm taking my knowledge back. No one will ever abuse it again."

The owl began flapping his wings and the

library started sinking into the desert.

Oh, no! He's destroying the library. And he's going to take us along with it!

We ran from the planetarium. But then I realized that we needed one more important piece of information: the date of the next eclipse.

"Sokka, let's go!" Katara called.

"If we leave this place we'll never get the infor—mation we need," I said. "Aang, come with me!"

While Katara and Momo tried to distract the owl, Aang and I hurried back to the planetarium. There we checked every day between now and the time that Sozin's Comet—the comet that will give the Fire Nation unlimited power—returns. In a few minutes we had the date. "That's it! The solar eclipse. It's just a few months away. Now let's get this info to Ba Sing Se!"

Aang and I met up with Katara and Professor Zei, who decided to stay and sink with the library. I think he's crazy for wanting to stay, but I guess he really loves to read. We, on the other hand, had to get out. Aang flew us back up the spire and out the window.

Toph had been holding up the building with

Earthbending! Once she saw that we were safe, she let it go and the entire library disappeared into the sand.

"We did it!" I yelled. "We got the information we need to stop the Fire Nation, and . . . where's Appa?"

That's when Toph told us that he was missing. Gone. Taken by a group of Sandbenders. And here we were in the middle of a desert, with no way out.

Big deal that we had the information that could stop the Fire Nation. What good would it do us if we never made it out of the desert?

Aang was furious. "How could you let them take Appa?" he shouted at Toph. "Why didn't you stop them?"

"I couldn't," she replied. "The library was sinking and you guys were still inside."

"I'm going after Appa," Aang declared, before taking off on his glider.

"Well, we'd better start walking," Katara suggested.

Why? What good would that do? We couldn't walk all the way to Ba Sing Se. We were doomed. There was no other way to look at it.

We walked on under the blazing sun. We got thirsty, but we had very little water. I found a cactus plant and drank some of its juice. Everything got a little fuzzy after that, and I really don't remember much about our journey across the desert. All I know is that we had to figure out a way to get to Ba Sing Se, and we had to try to find Appa.

After a while Aang returned without finding Appa. But we did find a sandsailing boardlike thing that Aang powered with Airbending. It was nice to know that we didn't have to walk all the way to Ba Sing Se.

As my head cleared we were attacked by a flock of flying buzzard–wasps. Nasty creatures. Luckily a group of Sandbenders came to our rescue, but then they wanted to know why we had a Sandbender sailer.

"Our bison was stolen," Katara explained. "We found this sailer in the desert."

"You dare accuse our people of theft when you ride on a stolen sandsailer!" one of the Sandbenders shouted.

"I recognize that voice," Toph whispered. "He's the Sandbender who took Appa."

"You stole Appa!" Aang screamed. "Where is he?"

And then Aang lost it. He blasted the Sandbenders' sand ships. That made the Sandbender confess.

"I didn't know he belonged to the Avatar," the frightened Sandbender said. "I traded him to some nomads. He's probably in Ba Sing Se by now. They were going to sell him there."

At that moment Aang went into the Avatar state. A huge wind funnel spun all around him. We had to get out of the way! I grabbed Toph and helped her run clear of the funnel. I looked around for Katara. Oh, no, what was she doing?

My sister actually walked toward Aang, right into the heart of the tornado that he had spun. Somehow she made it in and reached him. She hugged him, and slowly the winds died down.

Sometimes my sister is pretty amazing. But don't tell her I said that.

# Chapter 6

We needed to get to Ba Sing Se as quickly as possible to deliver our information. We left the desert and arrived at an area filled with lakes and waterfalls. According to the map I took from the library in the desert, there was only one way to get to the city.

"It looks like the only passage through all this water is a sliver of land called Serpent's Pass," I said.

Then a family of refugees showed up. They were also going to Ba Sing Se.

"Great," said Katara. "We can travel together through Serpent's Pass."

"Serpent's Pass?" one of the refugees said. "Only the truly desperate take that deadly route!"

"Deadly route," said Toph. "Great pick, Sokka."

Well, it didn't say "deadly route" on the map! We headed for the ferry instead.

At the ferry dock I felt a hand grab my collar. I turned to see a female security officer staring right at me.

"Is there a problem?" I asked, slightly annoyed.

"Yeah, I've got a problem with you," the guard said. "I've seen your type before. Sarcastic, think you're hilarious. And let me guess. You're traveling with the Avatar."

Whoa—who was this person? How did she know this about me? "Do I know you?" I asked suspiciously.

Then, of all things, she leaned in and kissed me! That's when I knew.

"Suki!" I yelled out.

"Hey, Sokka. It's so good to see you."

It was incredible to see Suki again. She is a Kyoshi warrior we met during our travels. And I really like her—a lot! It turned that out she had been working at the ferry helping refugees.

Just then someone stole the passports and tickets of the family of refugees we were traveling with, which meant they couldn't take the ferry.

"Don't worry," Aang said. "I'll lead you through Serpent's Pass."

Aw, Aang. Did we really have to do that? We gave up our tickets on the nice safe ferry to go on the deadly route for desperate people.

"I'm coming too," Suki said.

"Are you sure that's a good idea?" I asked, suddenly afraid that something might happen to her. It could be dangerous. She would probably be safer staying at the ferry dock.

"Sokka, I thought you'd want me to come," she said softly.

"I do. It's just—"

"Just what?"

"Nothing. I'm glad you're coming," I said with a smile. This trip just got a whole lot more complicated.

We arrived at the pass, which was a thin strip of land between two lakes—and were immediately attacked by Fire Nation ships patrolling the lake!

They lobbed a volley of fireballs at us. One of the fireballs hit the cliff above us and started a rockslide that headed right for Suki!

Dashing forward I pushed Suki out of the way. She fell clear of the tumbling rocks that somehow missed me, too.

"Suki! Are you okay? You have to be more careful!" I scolded. When I think that I could have lost her forever right then and there . . .

That night we set up camp, and I couldn't help worrying about Suki. She was putting her stuff really close to the edge! What was she

60 thinking? "You shouldn't sleep there," I said. "Who knows how stable this ledge is. It could give way at any moment."

"Sokka, I'm fine," she replied.

"You're right, you're right," I said. "You're perfectly capable of taking care of yourself." Maybe I was being overprotective. After all, she is a Kyoshi warrior.

"Wait!" I called out. Was that a spider crawling on her sleeping bag? Was it poisonous? What if it bit her in the middle of the night?

"Oh, never mind. I thought I saw a spider . . . but you're fine."

Suki didn't have anything to say, so I went to set up my own stuff and go to sleep. Except that I couldn't. There was too much to worry about. So I decided to take a walk, instead.

Apparently Suki couldn't sleep either—she was walking around, too.

"Look, I know you're just trying to help, but I can take care of myself," she told me.

"I know you can," I replied.

"Then why are you acting so overprotective?"

How could I explain this to her? Should I tell her about losing Yue?

"It's so hard to lose someone you care about," I said. "Something happened at the North Pole, and I couldn't protect someone. I don't ever want anything like that to happen again."

I have never stopped thinking about Princess Yue. I don't want to lose Suki like that.

And then Suki said something that threw me off guard. "I lost someone I cared about, too. He didn't die, he just went away. He was smart and brave and funny."

Well, how can I compete with a guy like that? "Who is this guy? Is he taller than me? Is he better looking?"

"It is YOU, stupid!" Suki said.

"Oh . . . ," I said, suddenly feeling really dumb. I guess I missed the point completely. Suki really cares about me! We looked into each other's eyes for a long moment. I feel so much for Suki—and yet I'm not sure how I should feel. Argh! Why do I have to think so much?

Then Suki leaned in to kiss me! What more could I want? Suki is great, and she thinks I'm smart and brave and funny. It's . . . it's . . . I couldn't. I had to back away.

"I'm sorry," Suki said, embarrassed.

62

"No, you shouldn't be," I replied, getting up and walking away instead of telling her why she didn't need to feel bad.

It's not you, Suki. It's me. I can't risk caring for somebody again. Not like I cared for Yue. It hurts too much when you lose them. It's not a chance I'm willing to take. I'm sorry, Suki. I'm really sorry.

⊕ ⊕ ⊕

The next day I found out why they call the route Serpent's Pass. A real-life giant sea serpent attacked!

As Aang and Katara battled the creature, Toph tumbled into the lake.

"Help! I can't swim!" she cried out. Then she vanished into the water.

"I'm coming, Toph!" I called out. I had to save her. I started to pull off my boots, and then—hey, Suki just dove right in with all her clothes on. She's a good swimmer, and she had no problem rescuing Toph. They're both okay. Whew! That's a relief. I would have saved Toph. I just wanted to get my boots off first.

Meanwhile, Aang and Katara finished off the sea serpent. (Good thing we have them around!) A short while later we came to the end of Serpent's Pass.

Aang took off to find Appa. "See you in the big city," he said.

Then Suki came up to me. "Sokka, it's been really great to see you again."

"Why does it sound like you're saying good-bye?" I asked.

"I came along to make sure you got through Serpent's Pass safely," she replied. "But now I have to get back to the other Kyoshi warriors."

What a dope I am. She was there to protect ME all along. No wonder she couldn't stand me acting so protective.

Then she started to apologize, "Listen, Sokka, I'm sorry about last night, I—"

Kiss her, Sokka. Just kiss her. "You talk too much," I said, before kissing her.

When we reached the outer wall of Ba Sing Se we were surprised to see Aang land beside us.

"What are you doing here?" Katara asked. "I thought you were looking for Appa."

"I was," said Aang. "But something stopped me. Something big."

Aang took us to the top of the outer wall, where we could see a huge scary-looking drill coming toward us. The Fire Nation was about to invade the city of Ba Sing Se!

We had to find a way to stop the invasion. Our first stop was the infirmary to visit some Earthbenders who had already gotten injured trying to stop the drill.

Katara examined an Earthbending captain. "His chi is blocked," she said. Then she asked him, "Who did this to you?"

"Two girls ambushed us," the captain replied. "One hit me with some quick jabs and suddenly I couldn't Earthbend anymore."

"Ty Lee!" Katara exclaimed. "She doesn't look dangerous, but she knows the human body and its weak points. It's like she takes you down from the inside."

And that's when I got my most brilliant idea yet. I knew how we could defeat that drill—by taking it down from inside.

We snuck onto the drill, and Aang and Katara started cutting away at its support braces with a whiplike Waterbending move.

Somehow I had envisioned it going a little faster, and as the two slowly made small cuts in the braces, I realized we would never cut through all of them in time. I had to figure out what more I could do.

But it was Aang who came up with an idea. "Maybe we don't need to cut all the way through each brace. If we weaken them all, I can deliver one big blow from above . . ."

Aha! I got it! "And BOOM! It all comes crashing down."

Aang and Katara started on Plan B, working quickly to make cuts in a series of braces. Just as they slashed the final brace,

Azula, Mai, and Ty Lee showed up.

"Guys, get out of here!" Aang shouted to us. "I know what I need to do!"

I heard Aang's command, but Ty Lee gave me a LOOK. I think she likes me. And I have to admit, she is cute. I mean, I know she's Fire Nation and all, but—

"Sokka!"

"Okay, Katara. I'm coming!" I yelled back. Sisters can be so annoying.

Katara and I climbed into a big pipe filled with slurry and rode the current, popping  out at the end of the tunnel. I knew it was just rocks and water mixed together, but it was still disgusting. It was in my mouth, eyes, ears—everywhere!

A few seconds later Ty Lee came out of the pipe, and Katara used Waterbending to trap her in the sludge. Then Aang slammed the drill from above and the whole thing collapsed.

We did it! We destroyed the Fire Nation drill!

"I just want to say, good effort out there today, Team Avatar," I told the others. Team Avatar. I like the sound of that. Now we're ready to head into Ba Sing Se!

# Chapter 7

We took the train from the outer wall into the city itself. There we were met by a woman who somehow knew who we were.

"Hello, my name is Joo Dee," she said. "I have been given the great honor of showing the Avatar around Ba Sing Se. And you must be Sokka, Katara, and Toph. Shall we get started?"

This was great. She'd know where the Earth King was. This was going to be easier than I imagined. "Yes," I said. "We have information about the Fire Nation that we need to deliver to the Earth King immediately."

"Great! Let's begin our tour, then I'll show you to your new home."

I was confused. Maybe she hadn't heard what I said, so I tried again. "We need to talk to the king about the war. It's important."

"You're in Ba Sing Se now. Everyone is safe here."

What was this lady's problem? It's like she was totally ignoring me—not to mention ignoring reality. She didn't realize how wrong she was. If we don't stop the Fire Nation, NOBODY will be safe anywhere.

But Joo Dee simply led us to a carriage and started our tour of the city. I tried to tell her again and again how important it was for us to see the king, but she ignored me each time.

"Maybe she's deaf?" I wondered out loud.

"She hears you," Toph said. "She's just not listening."

"Why won't she talk about the war?" Katara asked.

"Whatever her deal is, I don't like this place," Aang said. "We just need to find Appa and get out of here."

We passed the king's palace and saw some scary-looking guards. Joo Dee said that they were agents of the Dai Li, who guard the city's traditions.

"Can we see the king now?" Aang blurted out.

Joo Dee just laughed. "Oh, no. One doesn't just pop in on the king."

Now this was getting frustrating.

Then the carriage stopped in front of a really nice house.

"Here we are! Your new home!" Joo Dee said cheerfully, just as a messenger arrived with a scroll. She took it and read it quickly. Then she announced, "Good news! Your request to see the king is being processed and you should get to see him in about a month."

"A month!" We were going to have to stay in that weird place for a whole month? That wasn't going to leave us much time to prepare our attack on the Fire Nation.

"If we're going to be here for a whole month, we should spend our time looking for Appa," Aang said.

We searched all over the city. Not only had no one seen Appa, but everyone seemed scared to talk to us. Even our next-door neighbor was terrified.

"You can't mention the war here," he said. "And whatever you do, stay away from the Dai Li!"

I couldn't believe how crazy it was. Clearly we were not going to get help from anyone. Not from Joo Dee, not from our neighbors, and apparently not from the Dai Li. We were going to have to do it on our own. Which meant we needed a plan to get in to see the Earth King. He's the only one who could straighten everything out.

Later Katara saw something in the newspaper that gave her an idea. "The king is having a party at the palace tonight for his pet bear. We can sneak in with the crowd."

So that night, Katara and Toph dressed up as fancy ladies and went in first. Aang and I snuck in as busboys.

Then trouble came walking up to us. It was Joo Dee. "What are you doing here?" she wanted to know. "You have to leave immediately or we'll all be in terrible trouble."

I'd had it with her. "Not until we see the king!"

"You don't understand. You must go!"

But I wasn't about to leave. No one was going to tell us what to do. While Aang provided a distraction, I went to search for the king. A short while later he entered the ballroom. Then, as Aang rushed over to greet him, I was grabbed by two Dai Li guards and taken to a room along with Katara and Toph. A few minutes later Aang showed up with this guy Long Feng, the head of the Dai Li.

Ah, finally, someone who could give me some answers. "Why won't you let us talk to the king? We have information that could defeat the Fire Nation!"

"The Earth King has no time to get involved with political squabbles and the day-to-day minutia of military activities," Long Feng said.

"But this could be the most important thing he's ever heard!" Aang explained.

"What's most important to the king is maintaining the cultural heritage of Ba Sing Se. It's my job to oversee the rest of the city's resources, including the military."

So Long Feng was the guy who's really in power. This explained a lot.

"So the king is just a figurehead," Katara said.

"He's your puppet!" Toph added.

If this was the guy who's in charge, then maybe we'd come to the right place after all.

"We've found out about a solar eclipse that will leave the Fire Nation defenseless. You could lead an invasion—"

"Enough!" He angrily cut me off. "I don't want to hear your ridiculous plan. It is the strict policy of Ba Sing Se that the war not be mentioned within our walls."

It was all beginning to make sense. This guy had a sweet deal with all the power, and he was keeping the truth from the people of the city—not to mention from the king. This was corruption, plain and simple, and it was as bad as the Fire Nation itself.

"You can't keep the truth from all these people!" Katara shouted.

"I'll tell them," Aang said. "I'll make sure everyone knows."

"Until now you've been treated as honored guests," Long Feng said sternly. "But from now on you will be watched by Dai Li Agents. If you mention the war to anyone, you'll be expelled from the city."

He paused, watching our expressions before adding, "I understand you've been looking for your bison. It would be a shame if you were not able to complete your quest."

He's threatening us! He was going to kick us out before we had a chance to find Appa—and maybe he also knew where Appa was.

"Now Joo Dee will show you home," Long Feng said curtly before leaving.

A woman we had never seen before stepped into the room. "Come with me, please."

"What happened to Joo Dee?" Katara asked.

"I'm Joo Dee," the woman replied without hesitation.

Could this place get any weirder?

With our attempt to see the Earth King foiled, we turned our attention back to finding Appa. We put posters of the big furry guy up all over town, hoping that someone might have seen him. Shortly after we returned home the doorbell rang. It was Joo Dee—the first Joo Dee.

"Hello, Aang and Katara and Sokka and Toph," she said, smiling.

Of course she's smiling. She's always smiling. "What happened to you? Did the Dai Li throw you in jail?"

"Of course not! I simply took a short vacation to Lake Laogai, out in the country. It was quite relaxing."

"Why are you here?" Aang asked suspiciously.

Joo Dee pulled out one of our posters. "You are absolutely forbidden by the rules of the city to put up posters."

Great. Another thing that we're not allowed to do. We couldn't see the Earth King. We couldn't talk about the war. We couldn't put up posters. What good was it being here?

Aang was furious. "We don't care about the rules, and we're not asking permission! We're finding Appa on our own, and you should just stay out of our way!" Then he slammed the door in Joo Dee's face.

I winced. "That may come back to bite us in the blubber."

"I don't care," Aang said. "From now on we

do whatever it takes to find Appa."

"Yeah!" Toph agreed. "Let's break some rules!"

We headed back out to put up more posters and decided to split up to cover more ground. I took Toph with me. But it wasn't long before we heard a commotion coming from Katara's direction.

"Katara, what is it?" I asked.

"Jet's back," Katara answered before our eyes locked on the figure that was partly frozen and pinned to the wall behind her.

Jet was a rebel we met during our travels. He had done some pretty bad stuff, and Katara didn't trust him at all.

"I'm here to help you find Appa," he insisted. "I swear I've changed. I was a troubled person, and I let my anger get out of control. But I don't even have the gang now. I've put that all behind me."

"You're lying!" Katara said. Then Toph walked up to the wall and put her hand on it.

"He's not lying," she said. "I can feel his breathing and heartbeat. When people lie, there's a physical reaction. He's telling the truth."

"I heard two guys talking about some furry creature they had," Jet explained. "I figured it must be Appa."

Aang got all excited. "I bet they have Appa here in the city!"

Then we found out that Jet had been brainwashed by the Dai Li at their secret headquarters!

"Maybe Appa is in the same place they took Jet," Aang said hopefully. But Jet could not remember the name of the place.

"All I know is that it was under the water," Jet said. "Like under a lake."

That sounded familiar. "Remember what Joo Dee said?" I said. "She said she went on vacation to Lake Laogai."

"That's it!" Jet cried. "Lake Laogai!"

At last we had a lead to where Appa was. Now all we had to do was go there and rescue him!

# Chapter 8

Jet led us to the shores of Lake Laogai.

"So where are the secret headquarters?" I asked.

"Under the water, I think," Jet replied.

Toph felt around with her feet. "There's a tunnel right there near the shore." Using Earthbending, she opened the entrance and we slipped inside.

Beneath the lake we found a complex filled with hallways, rooms, and prison cells. We passed a group of women all being trained to be Joo Dee! It was definitely one of the creepiest things we had ever seen.

"I think Appa's in here," Jet said, when we came to one of the doors.

But when we stepped into the room, we didn't find Appa. Instead we found Long Feng and his Dai Li soldiers! Maybe Katara was right to be so wary of Jet. Maybe he did lead us all into a trap!

"By breaking into Dai Li headquarters you have made yourselves enemies of the state," Long Feng said.

Enemies of the state. I kind of liked the sound of that.

"Take them into custody!"

That didn't sound quite as good.

We battled the Dai Li, and Jet fought against them as hard as we did. There was no doubt that he was on our side.

"Long Feng is escaping!" Katara shouted.

Aang and Jet took off after him. Toph, Katara, and I stayed and finished off the Dai Li. When we caught up with the others, we found Aang kneeling over Jet, who was hurt. Long Feng was nowhere to be seen.

Katara tried healing Jet, but he ordered us to leave, insisting that he would be all right. We didn't want to leave him, but we had no choice.

We had to find Appa before it was too late.

We hurried to a large cell, hoping Appa would still be in there. But when we got there it was empty.

"Appa's gone!" Aang cried. "Long Feng beat us here!"

"If we keep moving maybe we can catch up with them!" I said.

Toph guided us through the maze of tunnels back up to the shore. There, Dai Li agents closed in on us from every side.

"We're trapped!" Katara shouted.

Then Momo suddenly got all excited and took off into the sky.

"What is it, Momo?" Aang asked.

I looked up and gasped. It was Appa!

We didn't know how he got free, but we didn't care. We were just glad to see him again.

That big furball wasted no time in helping us. He knocked down the Dai Li, then bit Long Feng in the leg and tossed him into the lake. Then we all climbed onto Appa's back and headed up into the sky.

It was just like old times.

We came to Ba Sing Se for two reasons—to find Appa and to tell the Earth King about the solar eclipse. It was more important than ever that we complete the second part of our mission. "Now's the time to tell the Earth King our plan. We're going to need his support if we want to invade the Fire Nation when the eclipse comes," I said.

"And now that we have Appa back, there's nothing to stop us from telling the Earth King the truth about the war and about Long Feng's conspiracy," Aang said.

 We flew back to the city and battled our way into the king's palace, fighting royal Earthbending guards who were trying to keep us out.

It was very strange—we were really on the same side, but we had to fight the guards as if they were the enemies, just for the chance to meet face-to-face with the king. I hoped it was worth it.

When we finally did reach the Earth King's throne room we found Long Feng by his side, along with some Dai Li agents and some royal Earthbending guards.

"We need to talk with you!" Aang told the Earth King.

Immediately Long Feng jumped in. "He's lying! They're here to overthrow you."

Overthrow the king? Well, that's really dumb. Why in the world would two people from the Water Tribe, an Earth Kingdom citizen, and the Avatar want to overthrow the leader of the Earth Kingdom? "No, we're on your side. We're here to help," I said.

"You have to trust us!" Katara added.

"You invade my palace, lay waste to all my guards, break down my fancy door, and you expect me to trust you?" the king replied.

"He has a good point," Toph said.

It was only when the king learned that Aang was the Avatar that he agreed at least to listen.

"There's a war going on right now—for the past one hundred years, in fact!" Aang explained. "The Dai Li have kept it a secret from you. It's a conspiracy to control the city and to control you!"

The king was really skeptical, but was willing to let us prove the conspiracy theory to him, so we boarded a train for Lake Laogai. And get this, we found out that the king had never been outside the palace before. Never! No wonder Long Feng could keep him in the dark about what was really going on in the world.

"Underneath Lake Laogai is the Dai Li's secret headquarters," I explained. "You're about to see where all the brainwashing and conspiring took place."

But when we arrived, the headquarters was gone.

"Oh, don't tell me!" I cried.

Katara and Toph used bending to try to find the opening, but it wasn't there. "There's nothing down there anymore," Toph said.

"I SAID 'don't tell me.'"

"The Dai Li must have destroyed the evidence," Katara said.

"This was a waste of my time!" the king said.

We had to think of something else. We finally had the Earth King's attention, but now we had nothing to show him. Or did we? "What about the drill?" I asked.

"That's it!" Katara cried. "They'll never be able to cover that up in time!"

We flew back to the city, and were relieved to see that the huge drill was still there.

"What is that?" the king asked when he saw it.

"A giant drill made by the Fire Nation to break through your walls," I explained. Now he would have to believe there's a war.

"This is nothing more than a construction project," someone said.

We all spun around to see Long Feng. He was still trying to convince the king we were lying.

"Then why is there a Fire Nation insignia on your construction project?" Katara asked.

That's my little sister. Sometimes she gets it right on the money! The king had Long Feng arrested and hauled off to jail. Justice is sweet!

Now that the Earth King knew we were telling him the truth, we could finally deliver the information we had worked so hard to get to him. "A solar eclipse is coming. The sun will be entirely blocked by the moon, and the Firebenders will be helpless," I said.

"What are you suggesting, Sokka?" the king asked.

"That the day we need to invade the Fire

Nation is the Day of the Black Sun."

"That would require moving troops out of Ba Sing Se. We'd be completely vulnerable."

He didn't get it, and I understood why. This was all new to him, and thinking of his city as anything other than a totally impenetrable fortress was foreign to him. But I had to convince him that he had no other choice.

"You're already vulnerable," I said. "The Fire Nation won't stop until Ba Sing Se falls. You can either sit back and wait for that to happen, or take the offensive and give yourself a fighting chance."

The Earth King thought for a few minutes. I could see that this was the most difficult decision he had ever had to make. "Very well. You have my support," he finally said.

Woo-hoo! We did it! We really might win this war after all! And things might actually get back to normal in the world.

As we were celebrating, General How, the leader of the Council of Generals, came into the throne room with some amazing news. "We've searched Long Feng's office. We've found some things that I believe will interest everybody. Long Feng kept secret files on everyone in Ba Sing Se, including you kids."

He had a letter from Toph's mother saying that she was here in the city and that she wanted to see Toph. He had a scroll that had been attached to Appa's horn when the Dai Li captured him. It was from a guru at the Eastern Air Temple—some kind of spiritual expert, according to Aang—who could help him take the next step in his Avatar journey.

But the best news of all came in the form of an intelligence report that a Water Tribe fleet was located near Chameleon Bay!

"It's Dad!" I couldn't believe it. Every day since we started our journey I've thought about seeing Dad again. Everything I do to help Aang, to help people fight the Fire Nation, I do to prove that I'm a warrior worthy of Dad's respect. And now, when things were finally looking up, we knew where he was. I had to go see him.

But then I remembered that someone needed to help the Earth King plan his invasion. I couldn't leave. Dad would have to wait.

Then Katara said something incredible. "No, Sokka," she said. "I know how badly you want to help Dad. You go. I'll stay here with the king."

She is the best sister ever! She was giving up the chance to see Dad so that I could fight by his side. I remember crying on the day he left for the war because he wouldn't take me with him. I've always believed that he thought I wasn't ready. Well, there's no more crying. I was finally a man, a true warrior of the Water Tribe. And soon I'd be fighting at his side. I couldn't remember when I'd felt happier!

As we all prepared to go our separate ways, news came that the Kyoshi Warriors were in the city.

"That means Suki's here!" I said. "I don't have time to see her now, but that sure gives me something to look forward to when I get back." After a long group hug, we said our good-byes.

Aang and I took off on Appa. He was going to drop me off at Chameleon Bay on his way to the Eastern Air Temple. As the city faded from view I couldn't help but smile at how things were finally looking up for us. The Earth King was on our side, Long Feng was in jail, and Suki would be waiting for me when I returned.

And best of all, I was going to see Dad!

# Chapter 9

Appa landed on a hill overlooking Chameleon Bay. I climbed down, glanced at the Water Tribe encampment below, and immediately felt nauseated. I didn't think I'd be so nervous seeing Dad again.

"You haven't seen your dad in more than two years," Aang said as he got ready to leave. "You must be so excited!"

"I know I should be, but I just feel sick to my stomach."

"Don't be nervous. He's going to be so happy to see you."

I nodded, even though in my heart I wasn't

sure. I watched as Aang flew away. "See you in a week!" he said. Then I was alone. I took a deep breath and started down the hill toward the camp.

I entered the camp and passed by some Water Tribe warriors.

I felt a little uncomfortable—they were staring at me like I didn't belong. . . . No, that wasn't it—they're staring at me because they recognized who I was. Then they came over to shake my hand!

Wow. I never expected a greeting like that! Maybe they heard about what I had been doing, or maybe it was just because of who my father is, but it sure felt good to be welcomed. One warrior pointed to a tent up ahead. Dad must be in there. If only he's as glad to see me as they were . . . well, here goes.

I stuck my head into the tent. Dad was there with his best friend, Bato, looking over a battle map. When Dad turned to look at me, his hard gaze met mine and I once again felt the power of his presence. Then his tough warrior's face softened and he smiled.

"Sokka," he said warmly.

He WAS glad to see me. I did make the right decision to come to him. "Hi, Dad!" I dashed across the tent and hugged him. And he hugged me back like neither one of us ever wanted to let go.

Over the next few days Dad helped me fit right in, just like I was one of the warriors who had left for battle with him all those years ago. I could see now that he was right to leave me behind at that time. I wasn't ready then, but I am now. Everything I have been through with Aang has made me the warrior I've become.

I got right to work helping Dad and his men set up a series of tangle mines along the bay to stop Fire Nation ships from getting to Ba Sing Se.

"The mines are filled with skunkfish and seaweed," Dad explained. "When a ship detonates the mine, the seaweed tangles up the propellers and the foul fish smell forces the crew to abandon ship. I call it the stink 'n' sink."

"Good one, Dad!" Stink 'n' sink! I can definitely see where I got my sense of humor!

Suddenly a warrior ran up to us. "Our scouts have spotted four Fire Nation ships."

"Bato, get these mines loaded up," Dad ordered. "The rest of you men, prepare for battle!"

What should I do? Should I go with the other men? I mean, even though I considered myself a warrior, I wasn't sure I was a warrior in Dad's eyes. Did he still see me as a little kid and expect me to stay behind? I didn't want to do the wrong thing. "Uh, what should I do, Dad?"

"Aren't you listening?" he said sternly. "I just said 'the rest of you men, prepare for battle!'"

He thinks I'm a man! I'm one of his warriors! I hurried to join the others, applied wolf battle paint to my face, strapped on my machete, and grabbed a war club.

90

"Ready to go knock some Fire Nation heads?" Dad asked.

"You don't know how much this means to me, Dad. I'll make you proud. And I'll finally prove to you what a great warrior I am."

Dad grasped my shoulder and squeezed gently. He looked right into my eyes and smiled. "Sokka, you don't have to prove anything to me. I'm already proud of you, and I've always known you're a great warrior."

"Really?"

"Why do you think I trusted you to look after our tribe when I left?"

Could this day get any better? I felt so proud—and so ready to fight the Fire Nation, right next to my father.

That's when Appa swooped down into our camp. And Aang's face said it all: the day had just turned bad. "This can't be good news," I said.

"Katara's in trouble," Aang said. "She needs our help."

I didn't need to hear any more. I hugged Dad tightly, then scrambled onto Appa's back and flew off. Looking down I could see the love in Dad's eyes as he watched me fly away. Then he turned and joined the other warriors on the Water Tribe ships setting out for battle. It felt good to know that he would have been proud to have me beside him on his ship.

"So what kind of trouble is Katara in?" I asked when the Water Tribe ships had faded from view.

"I don't know. In my vision I just knew she needed help."

Well, there was nothing to do but get back

to Ba Sing Se as fast as Appa could fly us.

Along the way we spotted Toph riding an Earthbending wave. We swooped down and picked her up.

"It was so great seeing my Dad again," I told her. "He treated me like a man, not a kid."

"I had a breakthrough myself," Toph told us. "I figured out how to bend metal."

"That's amazing, Toph! What about you, Aang?"

"I completely mastered the Avatar state."

It sounded like we'd all had pretty success—ful breaks—all except for Katara, apparently. I really hoped she was all right.

We landed in Ba Sing Se and hurried to the king's throne room.

"Katara's fine," the king told us. "She went off with the Kyoshi warriors."

Nothing to worry about—she's with Suki. But when we got back to our house we found Momo there by himself. He was agitated, jumping all over the place. She wasn't there. Maybe she really was in trouble.

Someone knocked at the door. When Toph

went to open it, I was shocked to see Zuko's uncle Iroh standing in the doorway!

"He's an old friend of mine," Toph said, before inviting him in.

I grabbed my war club. "I'm warning you. If you make one false move—"

"Princess Azula is in Ba Sing Se," Iroh said.

That's some really bad news.

"She must have Katara!" Aang said.

"She has captured my nephew as well."

"Then we'll have to work together to save Katara and Zuko," Aang announced.

Hold on—did I just hear Aang say we would work with Iroh to help save Zuko? That is SO wrong!

We then learned several things from a Dai Li agent Iroh had captured. "Azula is plotting to overthrow the Earth King," he told us. "And Katara and Zuko are in the crystal catacombs of Old Ba Sing Se, beneath the palace."

We hurried out to a courtyard near the palace, where Toph Earthbended a tunnel leading down.

We had two problems: We needed to

rescue Katara—and also that angry jerk Zuko—and we needed to warn the Earth King about Azula's coup. "I think we should split up," I said.

So Aang and Iroh headed down the tunnel while Toph and I went to warn the king. We spotted General How just in time to see a bunch of Dai Li agents surround and arrest him. "The coup has already started. We've got to get to the king right now!" I told Toph.

We burst into the throne room. There was the king surrounded by the Kyoshi warriors.

94

"Thank goodness we're in time!" I said. But something didn't feel right. I didn't recognize any of the girls. Where's Suki?

Then Ty Lee stepped forward and started flirting with me. While it was flattering and all, my heart was with Suki and—wait a second! What's going on?

"These aren't the real Kyoshi warriors!" Toph cried.

Ty Lee tried to block my chi but I managed to duck out of the way. That's when I saw that Azula was right next to the Earth King, ready to strike him with a Firebending move. We had no choice. We had to surrender or risk losing the king. The Dai Li hauled us away.

They locked Toph and me in an underground prison cell. The cell was made of metal, which they thought made it "Earthbender proof." But they had no idea that Toph had learned to bend metal. . . . Hey, if you're going to be locked in a metal prison cell, it's a good idea to have a Metalbender with you.

"See any Dai Li agents nearby?" Toph asked.

"Nope," I whispered. "All clear."

Toph bent open the metal bars of the cell and we stepped right through. After knocking down a few Dai Li guards, we hurried to the Earth King's cell. Toph did her Metalbending thing again and freed the king. "Come on, we've got to get you to safety!" I told him.

We rushed back through the tunnels and ran into Katara. In her arms she held Aang. His eyes were closed and he wasn't moving.

"Oh, no." What happened to Aang? He had to be all right. All of this meant nothing if Aang wasn't okay.

I had a million questions for Katara, but I

knew that getting out of Ba Sing Se was more important right then.

We returned to the surface and found Appa. Then Katara, Aang, Toph, the Earth King, and I took off. Once we were safely in the air, Katara used her Waterbending healing ability to help Aang. He opened his eyes and, although he was weak and groggy, it looked like he was going to be okay.

As we flew over the outer wall of Ba Sing Se, soaring away from the city, the Earth King looked down and said, "The Earth Kingdom has fallen."

Until that very moment it hadn't really hit me. The Earth King was leaving his city. Azula's coup attempt was successful. The Fire Nation now had control of Ba Sing Se, and with it, the entire Earth Kingdom.

We failed. I failed. What good is our information about the Fire Nation now? How in the world can we stop them? Will I ever see Dad again? Will anything ever go back to being normal? I wish I knew, but at the moment, I just don't have a clue.